Nibble, Nibble, Jenny Archer

by Ellen Conford

Illustrated by Diane Palmisciano

Little, Brown and Company

Boston   New York   Toronto   London

First Edition

The characters and events in this book are fictitious. Any simi-
larity to real persons, living or dead, is coincidental and not in-
tended by the author.

Library of Congress Cataloging-in-Publication Data

Conford, Ellen.
    Nibble, nibble, Jenny Archer / by Ellen Conford ;
illustrated by Diane Palmisciano.—1st ed.
        p.   cm.—
    Summary: Jenny Archer is excited about making a television
commercial for a new snack food, until she discovers that the
food she liked so much was meant for gerbils.
    ISBN 0-316-15371-0
    [1. Television advertising—Fiction.   2. Humorous
stories.]   I. Palmisciano, Diane, ill.   II. Title.
PZ7.C7936Ni 1993
[Fic]—dc20   92-34306

10 9 8 7

WOR

*Published simultaneously in Canada
by Little, Brown & Company (Canada) Limited*

1

Jenny Archer was getting bored waiting for Mrs. Wynn to finish her shopping.

"Your mother is taking an awfully long time in there," she told her friend Wilson. Jenny looked at the entrance to Wide World of Toys and sighed.

"She must be getting me a lot of birthday presents," Wilson said hopefully.

Jenny and Wilson were supposed to be taking care of Wilson's baby brother. But Tyler had fallen asleep in his stroller ten minutes ago. Jenny almost wished that he'd wake up, so she'd have something to do.

But the busy shoppers at the mall didn't seem to bother Tyler a bit.

"Look over there." Wilson pointed to a small table next to a planter of artificial trees. "I didn't notice that before."

"Neither did I," said Jenny. "Let's go see what it is."

"Maybe they're giving away free samples," said Wilson.

Once Jenny and Wilson had seen a woman at the mall in a bee costume. She was handing out samples of a new candy bar called Honey Bunch Crunch. It wasn't very good candy, but it was free. Maybe this time there would be free ice cream.

Jenny pushed the stroller toward the table. Wilson darted ahead of her. A woman with short dark hair stood behind the table.

She was filling up little paper dishes with something from a big box.

"Is it ice cream?" Jenny asked.

"No," said Wilson, disappointed. "It looks like cereal."

The woman smiled at them. "It's a new product," she said. "It's a special sort of food."

"What kind of food?" asked Wilson.

"Something different," the woman said. "Something unusual." She pushed one of the paper dishes at Wilson. "Would you like to try it?"

Wilson looked into the little dish. "I don't like unusual foods," he said.

"I do," said Jenny. She was older than Wilson. She had more grown-up tastes. "I'll try it."

The woman handed her the paper dish. It was filled with a mixture of brown, green, and yellow pellets. It looked a little like trail mix, but the pieces were smaller.

"It must be a new snack food," Jenny said.

The woman just smiled.

Jenny wasn't sure she liked snack foods colored brown, green, and yellow. Unless they were M&M's.

She picked up a few pieces. She put them carefully on her tongue. Whatever this new food was, it certainly was unusual. She chewed thoughtfully. She had never tasted anything like it.

"This really is different." She scooped up some more of the pellets. She popped them in her mouth.

"I like it," she said. "Some of it's crunchy and some of it's soft. And it's all interesting flavors."

She held the dish out to Wilson. "You have to try this."

Wilson looked down at the food. He frowned. He picked up one little yellow pellet. He closed his eyes and stuck it in his mouth.

"Eww!" He made a horrible face. "This is weird. What is this stuff?"

4

The woman behind the table looked disappointed.

Jenny shook the last bits from the dish into her mouth. She wasn't absolutely sure she loved the new food. But she didn't want to hurt the woman's feelings.

"I think it's delicious," Jenny said. "It's probably meant for grown-ups."

The dark-haired woman began to smile again. "Not really. But it's full of vitamins. It's very healthy."

"Delicious *and* nutritious," Jenny said. "I'm going to ask my mother to buy me some."

"That's it!" a voice cried out from behind a plastic tree. "Perfect!"

Jenny whirled around. A young woman in jeans was climbing out of the planter. She was followed by a man with a clipboard.

" 'I'm going to ask my mother to buy me some!' " the man repeated. " 'Delicious *and* nutritious!' I love this kid!"

The woman in jeans was holding a video camera. She was laughing. "Everyone's going to love her."

"Were you taping me?" Jenny asked. "What's going on?"

"Have you ever been on TV?" the man asked.

Jenny shook her head.

"Well, you're going to be," he said. "Young lady, you are the star of the first Nibble Nibble TV commercial."

2

"TV commercial?" Jenny was so excited she could hardly talk. "Me? Star?"

Now everyone was smiling at her. Except Wilson. He was staring. His eyes were wide. His mouth was open in an O of surprise.

The man pulled a sheet of paper from his clipboard. "Your parents will have to sign this release." He handed Jenny the piece of paper.

"What's a release?" she asked.

"It's a legal form," he said. "It gives us the right to use you in our commercial. If we pay you a certain amount of money."

"You're going to pay me?" Jenny said. "I'm going to be on TV and get money, too?"

The man nodded.

Wilson's eyes grew even wider.

"How much money?" Suddenly pictures began to form in Jenny's head. She was lying near a swimming pool, wearing sunglasses. She held a cordless phone in one hand. With the other, she fed an apple to her new palomino pony. "Yes," she was saying to her friend Beth. "I miss you, too. But I do love it out here in Hollywood."

"A lot of money?" she asked.

"Well," said the man, "not enough to buy a Cadillac."

The swimming pool in Jenny's imagination dried up.

"Enough to buy a pony?" she asked hopefully.

The three grown-ups laughed.

"She's great," said the woman with the

camera. "A natural."

"She is," the dark-haired woman agreed. "I love her enthusiasm."

The man pulled out a business card and handed it to Jenny. "Have your parents call me," he said. "You might get that Cadillac yet."

"You want me to make more commercials?" Jenny filled her imaginary swimming pool again. The blue-green water sparkled in the sun.

"You never know," said the man. "By the way, what's your name?"

"Jenny Archer."

He wrote it down on his clipboard.

"But I could change it for TV," she added.

"Don't change a thing, honey," said the woman in jeans. "Stay just the way you are."

Finally Wilson said something. "Am I going to be in the commercial, too?"

The man shook his head. "I'm afraid not," he said. "You didn't like Nibble Nibble."

"Let me taste it again," Wilson said. "I'm sure I'll like it this time."

"Sorry," the man said.

Wilson looked so disappointed that Jenny was afraid he might cry.

"Don't feel bad," she said to him. "They use kids in lots of commercials. When I do my next one, I'll ask for you to be in it with me."

Wilson brightened up. "You will?" He clapped his hands. The three grown-ups began to laugh again. Jenny didn't know why, but she didn't have time to find out.

"Wahhhh!"

At last, Tyler had woken up.

Jenny bent down. Quickly she lifted Tyler from his stroller. At the same moment, Mrs. Wynn rushed toward them. Her arms were full of packages.

"You were supposed to wait outside the store!" she scolded.

"Wahhhh!" yelled Tyler. Jenny cuddled

him against her shoulder and patted his back.

"What are you doing over here?" Mrs. Wynn asked.

"Making a TV commercial!" Jenny's eyes glowed. "My *first* TV commercial. Mrs. Wynn, do you think Tyler would be scared to ride a pony?"

3

Jenny's mother and father were in the kitchen when she came home. They were sitting at the table, writing out checks.

"I'm going to be on TV!" she yelled as she ran into the room. "I'm going to be in a commercial! Maybe *lots* of commercials!"

Her mother looked up from the checkbook, startled. "Really?"

"Really!" Jenny said. "And they're going to give me money."

Her father tore open an envelope. "Enough

to pay the electric bill?" he asked.

"I don't know," Jenny said. "Maybe—if it costs less than a Cadillac."

He pulled the bill out of the envelope. "Not much less," he said glumly.

Jenny wondered why her parents weren't as excited as she was. "Are we poor?" she asked, worried.

"No, no," her mother said quickly. The last time Jenny thought they were poor, she had tried to sell their house. "We only *feel* poor when we're paying bills."

"Are you sure you're not getting carried away again?" her father asked. "You know, sometimes you can be a little—"

"I *am* going to be in commercials," Jenny insisted. "At least, I'm going to be in *one* commercial."

She pulled out the card the man at the mall had given her and handed it to her father. "See? You have to call this man. He'll tell you how much they're going to pay me."

Her father read the card out loud. "Bizmark Productions. TV, radio, magazines, newspapers. Arthur Mark."

Mrs. Archer leaned over to read the card herself. "It looks real," she said.

"It is real." Jenny pulled the release form out of her other pocket. "And you have to sign this."

Her mother was puzzled. "But how did you happen to do a commercial?" she asked.

Jenny sighed happily. "It's a long story," she said.

And she sat down at the kitchen table and told it to them.

Jenny insisted that her father call Bizmark Productions right away.

"It's in the city," said Mr. Archer. "Mr. Mark won't even be back at his office yet."

"He could be," Jenny said. "If he took a helicopter."

"Jenny, you *are* getting carried away," said Mrs. Archer.

"They said I was a natural. Doesn't that mean I was good?"

Her father eyed her, his face thoughtful. He studied the release form Jenny had given him. He looked over at Mrs. Archer. "Maybe she's not getting carried away."

He picked up the phone.

The people Jenny had met at the mall were not back in the office yet. But Jenny's father spoke to someone else who worked for Bizmark.

When he hung up the phone, he looked dazed.

"Did they tell you how much money I'm going to make?" Jenny asked.

"She couldn't say exactly," Mr. Archer replied. "But she said a normal fee would be around five hundred dollars."

"*Five hundred dollars!*" Jenny jumped

straight up in the air. *"Yes!"* she yelled.

"Five hundred dollars?" her mother repeated. She looked as if she might jump straight up in the air, too.

"And that's just for one commercial!" Jenny exclaimed. "It didn't even take five minutes. That's a hundred dollars a minute!"

Her father came back to the table. He picked up the electric bill. He still had that dazed look on his face.

But Jenny didn't notice. She was too busy leaping around the kitchen. "Five hundred dollars!" she sang. "Five hundred dollars!"

"Um, Jenny?" Her father cleared his throat.

Jenny bounced over to him. She looked like she was on a pogo stick. "Yes?" she asked, still bouncing.

"Could you lend us ninety-two dollars and thirty-three cents?"

4

"That is so amazing," said Jenny's friend Beth. It was Monday morning. Jenny, Beth, and Wilson were walking to school.

"Things like that never happen to me," she went on.

"It was just good luck," said Jenny. "I was in the right place at the right time."

"I was in the same place at the same time," Wilson said gloomily, "and it didn't happen to me."

"Well, it will," said Jenny. "As soon as I get to do another commercial."

"Five hundred dollars," Beth said, "for five minutes' work. You know, Jenny, you could make an awful lot of money at this."

They reached the school corner. The crossing guard held up her hand.

"You really could," said Wilson. "Even if you only made one commercial a month, that would be—" He tried to figure it out.

"Six thousand dollars a year!" Beth said.

The guard signaled for them to cross the street.

Jenny couldn't move.

"Six thousand dollars?" she said. "Six *thousand* dollars?"

She tried to think of a good name for a pony.

"And if you made two commercials a month—" Beth began.

"*Twelve* thousand dollars!" Jenny cried.

The crossing guard blew her whistle. She waved her arm at them. But Jenny still didn't move.

"And I could easily make one a week," she said. "Even if it took more than five minutes."

"That's twenty-four thousand dollars!" Beth shrieked.

For a moment, Jenny felt dizzy. Twenty-four thousand dollars! And that was just for her first year!

The crossing guard started to yell: "Are you kids going to stand there all day, or what?"

Beth tugged at Jenny's arm. Jenny hardly felt it. Another picture was forming in her mind.

She was sitting in front of her new, forty-six-inch giant-screen TV. She was watching one of her commercials. In the kitchen, her parents were paying bills.

They were whistling as they wrote out the checks.

*　　*　　*

Every Monday Jenny's class went to the school library. Sometimes Ms. Greenberg, the librarian, gave them a lesson on using the library.

Today they would have a quiet reading period. The rest of the class began to choose books. But all Jenny could think of was being a commercial star.

The library has books about everything, Jenny reminded herself. Maybe there's a book about acting in commercials. Jenny asked Ms. Greenberg.

"Let's check," said Ms. Greenberg. She led Jenny over to the "Careers" section. She searched the shelves, and pulled out a book.

There it was! *How to Make Big Money in TV Commercials.*

Jenny hugged the book to her chest. Then she ran to a table and started to read.

5

Jenny thought that *How to Make Big Money in TV Commercials* was the most interesting book she'd ever read. She couldn't put it down.

She read all the way through library period.

She read while she ate lunch. Beth told everyone about how Jenny was going to be on TV. Jenny hardly heard the excited questions the kids asked her.

She was up to the chapter called "Do You Have What It Takes to Be a Commercial Star?"

"Enthusiasm is vital," the book said. "You must be excited about the product you are selling."

I have lots of enthusiasm, Jenny thought. I get enthusiastic about almost everything. The lady at the mall said she loved my enthusiasm.

"Energy is a must," the book went on. "You should be lively and energetic."

I have tons of energy, Jenny thought. And I'm lively. Sometimes her parents even thought she was too lively.

She was still reading as she walked home from school.

"Casting directors are looking for the 'Kid Next Door' type. You should be natural, but with a little extra sparkle."

The woman at the mall had said Jenny was a natural.

"So be yourself," read Jenny. "Turn on the energy and sparkle, sparkle, sparkle!"

By the time she got home, she could feel herself almost exploding with energy.

"HI, MRS. BUTTERFIELD!" Mrs. Butter-field took care of Jenny when her parents were at work. "ISN'T IT A FANTASTIC DAY?"

"Why are you yelling?" Mrs. Butterfield asked.

"I'M NOT YELLING!" Jenny said. "I'M BEING ENTHUSIASTIC!"

Barkley, Jenny's big black dog, cocked his head to one side. He didn't understand what Jenny was saying. But to him it sounded like yelling.

"What are you so enthusiastic about?" asked Mrs. Butterfield.

"EVERYTHING! I'M JUST A NATU-RALLY ENTHUSIASTIC PERSON! AND I HAVE TONS OF ENERGY, TOO!"

Mrs. Butterfield rolled her eyes. "Would you please use some of your energy to take Barkley for a walk?"

"A WALK! WHAT A GREAT IDEA! COME ON, BARKLEY! WE'LL HAVE A WONDERFUL WALK!"

Barkley eyed Jenny curiously. She took him for a walk every afternoon. But she wasn't usually so loud about it.

"A WALK WILL BE INTERESTING AND FUN!" she said. "MAYBE WE'LL STOP AND VISIT BETH! WON'T THAT BE DELIGHTFUL?"

"Jenny," said Mrs. Butterfield, "I don't know why you're screaming. But could you please lower your voice?"

"I'm not screaming," Jenny said. But she lowered her voice. A little. "I'm *sparkling*."

Mrs. Butterfield got up from the couch. She went into the kitchen and got Barkley's leash. She handed it to Jenny.

"Here," she said. "Go sparkle outside."

6

"BOW-WOW BURGERS WITH BACON BITS!" Jenny told Barkley. She showed him the package. "WHEAT FLOUR, BEEF, SOY GRITS, GROUND COOKED BACON. ANIMAL FAT, FOLIC ACID . . ."

Barkley danced around her feet, tail wagging. He was eager for his supper. Usually Jenny just tore open two packets of burgers and put them in his dish.

But tonight she was shouting about his food instead of giving it to him.

29

She opened the box and took out one burger. She held it up. Barkley stood on his hind legs, trying to reach it.

"DOGS LOVE BOW-WOW BURGERS WITH BACON BITS BECAUSE THEY'RE TAIL-WAGGING, LIP-SMACKING GOOD!"

"Jenny," her father said, "why are you yelling about dog food?"

"I'm not yelling," she said. "I'm practicing."

"Practicing what?" her mother asked.

"I'm practicing being enthusiastic. I read a book about doing TV commercials. You have to sparkle, sparkle, sparkle."

"Being enthusiastic," her father said, "is one thing you don't need to practice."

Barkley trotted to his food dish. He trotted back to Jenny. He shoved his head under her arm.

"And you're driving Barkley crazy," her mother pointed out.

"I'm just trying to tell him how good Bow-Wow Burgers are," said Jenny.

"He doesn't know what you're trying to tell him," Mrs. Archer said. "He just thinks you're teasing him."

"Oh, I didn't mean to do that." Jenny quickly unwrapped two Bow-Wow Burgers. She put them in Barkley's dish. "Here, Barkley. I'll practice on something else."

Barkley wolfed down the burgers before Jenny could take them back.

Jenny and her parents sat down to their own dinner.

"TUNA CASSEROLE!" Jenny exclaimed. "GOOD, AND GOOD FOR YOU, TOO! FRESH CANNED TUNA, CREAMY EGG NOODLES, AND A GOLDEN BROWN TOPPING OF BREAD CRUMBS."

She took a forkful. "OH, BOY! I WISH WE COULD HAVE THIS FOR DINNER EVERY NIGHT!"

"I wish we could have a quiet dinner to-night," her father said.

Mrs. Archer gave her a curious look. "You were never that crazy about tuna casserole, Jenny."

"I'm sparkling," she reminded her mother. "I have to sound like I love the stuff I'm advertising."

Her father looked up from his salad. "Even if you don't love it?"

"But I like almost everything," said Jenny. "Except anchovies."

Mr. Archer turned to Jenny's mother.

"Let's have anchovies for dinner tomor-row night."

For the next two weeks, Jenny practiced commercials for everything. As she brushed her teeth, she told the mirror how bright her smile was.

"That's because I use fresh-tasting Dazzle-

Mint toothpaste."

Her mother asked her to go to Mr. Marvel's deli to buy some milk. But she didn't just ask for a container of milk. She told Mr. Marvel she wanted a quart of his dairy-fresh, calcium-rich, Vitamin D–fortified milk.

One day in school Mrs. Pike asked her to clean the blackboard. Jenny picked up the eraser and began to tell the class what a fine eraser it was. "NINE OUT OF TEN TEACHERS AGREE! THEY WOULD RATHER USE WIPE-WRITE ERASERS THAN ANY OTHER BRAND!"

Jenny was driving everyone crazy with her sparkling.

And she was practically going crazy herself. When would her commercial be on TV? It had been weeks since the Archers mailed back the release. But no one from Bizmark Productions had called yet.

Jenny began to believe that her commercial

would never be on television. But one Monday afternoon Mrs. Butterfield was waiting for her at the front door.

"They called!" she said. "Your commercial is going to be shown on Thursday! At 7:14 P.M., during *Dialing for Dollars!*"

"Yay!" Jenny leapt straight up in the air. Her feet hardly touched the ground before she shot down the street toward Beth's house.

7

The next morning, Mrs. Pike let Jenny announce that her commercial was to be aired on Thursday. At lunchtime Jenny visited every table in the cafeteria.

"Be sure to watch me on TV Thursday."

At three o'clock she stopped in front of the school buses. "Don't forget to watch me on Thursday," she told the kids as they boarded their buses. "*Dialing for Dollars*. Seven-fourteen P.M."

She was too excited to practice anymore. All she could do was count the hours until she could see herself on TV.

Thursday night, Beth and Wilson came over after dinner. Mrs. Butterfield stayed late, too. They all wanted to watch *Dialing for Dollars* with the Archers.

Jenny was too nervous to eat dinner. By the time seven o'clock came, her heart was pounding like a kettle drum.

Dialing for Dollars was a game show. The players had to make words out of the letters on the telephone dial. Sometimes Jenny played along, and tried to figure out the answers. But tonight all she could do was watch the clock.

"I can't stand it!" she moaned as the game started.

"Me neither," said Beth.

"What time is it?" Wilson asked.

"Four minutes after seven," said Mr. Archer.

"I think the answer is President Nixon,"

said Mrs. Butterfield.

"What time is it now?" Jenny asked.

"Four and a half minutes after seven," her father answered.

"I'll never make it," she said.

"We've waited this long," Mrs. Archer said. "We can certainly wait a few more minutes." She folded her hands in her lap. She tried to look calm.

But suddenly she jumped up from the couch. "We don't care what the answer is!" she yelled at the TV set. "Get to the commercial!"

And at last, they did.

"We're here at this busy mall," an announcer said. "To do a taste test for a new product."

"There you are!" said Jenny's mother.

Jenny clasped her hands together. She held her breath. She recognized her red-and-white striped shirt. But it was hard to believe she was really seeing herself on TV.

"You look great!" said Beth.

"And we're about to play a little trick on this young lady," the announcer went on.

"A trick?" Jenny frowned. "What do they mean?"

"We're doing a taste test," the announcer explained, "for a new gerbil food."

"GERBIL FOOD!" Jenny shrieked.

"Gerbil food?" her father echoed.

"What a dirty trick!" said Mrs. Butterfield. The camera focused on Jenny's face. She was popping the yellow and brown pellets into her mouth.

Jenny stared at the screen, stunned.

Mrs. Archer shook her head. "I don't understand this. Why did they use you? Why didn't they get a gerbil?"

Jenny was too shocked to talk. But the Jenny on TV was speaking. "I like it. Some of it's crunchy and some of it's soft. And it's all interesting flavors."

"I can't believe it," said the real Jenny. "It

didn't taste like gerbil food."

"How do you know?" asked Wilson. "You never tasted gerbil food before."

"Shh!" said Beth.

"Yes," the announcer went on. "Nibble Nibble Gerbil Kibble combines all the nutrients gerbils need and love. Alfalfa meal, whole oats, dried beet pulp, flaked corn, and sunflower seeds."

"Good grief," Jenny's father said.

"What's dried beet pulp?" asked Wilson.

"Shh!" said Beth.

The camera zoomed in on a close-up of Jenny's face. "Delicious *and* nutritious," said the Jenny on TV. "I'm going to ask my mother to buy me some."

"Gerbil food," the real Jenny muttered. She stared at herself on the screen. "I can't believe it was gerbil food."

The announcer was speaking again. "If this little girl loves Nibble Nibble Gerbil Kibble—"

"I didn't love it," Jenny protested. "I said it was interesting."

"—imagine how much your gerbil will love it," the announcer said.

Another close-up of Jenny's face filled the TV screen. Again she said, "I'm going to ask my mother to buy me some."

"Sorry, young lady," the announcer finished. "We know you like it. But it's for gerbils."

Jenny's face faded from the screen. *Dialing for Dollars* came back on. For a moment there was absolute silence in the Archers' living room.

Then Beth started to clap. Wilson jumped up on the couch and yelled, "Yay, Jenny!" Mrs. Butterfield gave her a hug.

"Even if it was a dirty trick," she said, "you were very good."

"Don't you think I looked dumb?" Jenny asked. "Eating gerbil food?"

"You looked adorable," her mother said.

"You didn't look dumb at all," said her father. "You sparkled."

"But I sparkled for gerbil food," Jenny said.

"That's what doing commercials is all about," her father reminded her. "You said so yourself. You have to be enthusiastic about what you're selling."

"I guess so," Jenny said slowly.

"I think those TV people were right," said Mrs. Butterfield. "You're a natural. I'll bet they'll ask you to do more commercials."

"Do you think so?" Jenny asked.

"Definitely," said Beth. "And this will make a great story when you get interviewed for *People* magazine."

Jenny closed her eyes. Her imagination went to work. She pictured herself talking to a woman with a notebook.

"How did you get to be such a success in TV commercials?" the woman was asking her.

"Well," Jenny said, "believe it or not, I ate

a dish of gerbil food."

"That's marvelous!" The woman scribbled in her notebook. "Our readers are going to love this. Tell me all about it."

Jenny opened her eyes. "Maybe you're right," she said to Beth. "It would make an interesting story."

"And think of your five hundred dollars," Wilson reminded her. "I bet you could buy a pony for five hundred dollars."

"Wow!" said Jenny. "I bet I could."

"No, she can't!" snapped Mr. Archer.

"Not even a very small pony?" Jenny asked hopefully.

8

When Jenny walked into the school yard the next morning, a mob of kids gathered around her.

They all began to shout questions.

"Was that *really* gerbil food you ate?"

"Did it really taste good?"

"What's dried beet pulp?"

"How could you eat that stuff? Eee-eww!"

"I didn't know it was gerbil food," Jenny said.

Howard Berry stuck his front teeth over his

lip, like a rabbit. He made smacking sounds. "Nibble, nibble," he said. "Nibble, nibble, Jenny."

Some of the kids started to laugh.

"I don't think that's funny, Howard," Jenny said.

"Nibble, nibble," he repeated. "Nibble, nibble, Jenny Archer eats gerbil kibble. Hey, I made a poem!"

"It's a stupid poem," Jenny said angrily.

Clifford Stern began chanting it, too. "Nibble, nibble, nibble, nibble, Jenny Archer eats gerbil kibble!"

"Cut it out!" she shouted.

But suddenly a whole bunch of boys were singing it. "Nibble, nibble, nibble, nibble, Jenny Archer eats gerbil kibble!"

Jenny whirled around and marched away from them. She held her head high and her back straight. But there were tears in her eyes.

In class Jenny had to do an arithmetic

problem at the board. Howard whispered to her as she walked past his desk. "Nibble, nibble, Jenny."

She bit her lip and pretended to ignore him.

But she made a mistake in the problem. Mrs. Pike had to correct her. She walked back to her desk, feeling angry that she'd let Howard upset her.

She walked by Clifford Stern. He whispered at her. "Better start eating people food. Before your brain gets gerbil size."

"Even if it does," she whispered back, "it'll still be bigger than yours."

At lunch Jenny sat with Beth and April Adams and Sarah Faith. Sarah and April didn't tease her. They were excited about seeing her on television.

"You looked just like yourself," Sarah said. "But you sounded like a real professional commercial actress."

"That's funny," said Jenny. "They said they

liked me because I sounded natural."

"I guess you're just naturally professional," April said.

Jenny started to feel much better.

Until Howard and Clifford came to their table.

"What are you eating today, Jenny?" asked Clifford. "Hamster food?"

"Nah," said Howard. "I know what she's eating. Mosquito eyes and alfalfa sprouts. And sunflower seeds and turtle snouts."

Sarah giggled. April tried not to. Beth glared at Howard.

Howard and Clifford laughed so hard they nearly fell over the lunch table.

When Jenny got home that afternoon, she could still hear the chants of "Nibble, nibble" in her ears.

While her parents were making dinner, she told them what had happened at school.

"Kids are mean sometimes," her mother

said. "They don't stop to think how it feels to be teased."

"Grown-ups can be mean, too," Jenny said. "Like Mr. Mark and that lady. They tricked me into eating gerbil food. They didn't care if people laughed at me."

"Jenny, the kids will stop teasing you after a while," her father said. "And who knows? Maybe Mr. Mark will ask you to do another commercial. For something else."

"I'm not going to do any more commercials," Jenny said bitterly. "Commercials are dumb. And the people that make them are big liars. And I'm never going to speak to Mr. Mark again."

"Well, let's forget about it for now." Her mother tried to sound cheerful. "We're having something new for dinner tonight."

"What?" asked Jenny.

"California burgers," her mother said.

"What are California burgers?" Jenny asked.

"They're hamburgers. Topped with avocado slices and alfalfa sprouts."

"*Alfalfa* sprouts!" Jenny cried. "*Alfalfa? How could* you?*"

She burst into tears and ran out of the kitchen.

9

Jenny's commercial was on *Dialing for Dollars* again Friday night. And it ran every night for the whole next week.

Howard and Clifford kept chanting, "Nibble, nibble" at her. At first, Jenny tried to make up nasty poems of her own.

"Howard, Howard, big fat coward. An ox in the zoo is smarter than you."

And, "Clifford, Clifford, Clifford Stern. You make everyone's stomach turn."

But her poems didn't seem to bother them.

And Jenny had never practiced being mean. She was not a natural at picking on people.

Instead she started picking on commercials. Every time the Archers watched television, Jenny yelled at the TV.

"ELMO FENTON OF MUNCIE, INDIANA, GREW THIS EIGHT-POUND CUCUMBER USING VEG-A-MIRACLE PLANT FOOD!" the commercial claimed.

"What a fake," Jenny said. "I bet that's not even a cucumber. That's a skinny watermelon."

"YOU CAN LOSE FIVE POUNDS A WEEK ON THE MIAMI MIRACLE DIET PLAN! JUST HAVE A DELICIOUS MIAMI LIQUID SHAKE FOR BREAKFAST AND LUNCH. THEN EAT A SENSIBLE DINNER."

"Sure," said Jenny. "Two peas and a carrot."

"HONEY BUNCH CRUNCH! THE CANDY WITH A YUM IN EVERY BAR!"

"And a yuck in every bite," Jenny added.

"Jenny," her father said finally. "You're right not to believe everything you see in commercials. But aren't you getting a little too worked up over this?"

"I don't believe *anything* I see in commercials," Jenny said. "Those people tricked a kid into eating gerbil food. Why should you trust them to ever tell the truth?"

"I've never seen you so angry," her mother said. "The people at Bizmark didn't set out to hurt you. They liked you."

"Well, I don't like them."

"Aren't you ever going to forgive them?" asked her father.

"Maybe," said Jenny. "When they stop showing my commercial. And when Howard and Clifford stop making fun of me."

On Saturday morning, Jenny was watching *Crazy Critter Cartoons* on TV. There were lots of commercials to yell at.

54

"AWESOME ACKMACK THE ANDROID! FROM THE PLANET MERCURY! MELTS HIS ENEMIES WITH THE DEADLY LASER-LOBBER!"

"He's two inches high!" Jenny retorted. "He's plastic. He'd melt *himself*. And nobody lives on Mercury!"

Her mother came into the living room. She was holding the mail. "Look, Jenny." She handed her an envelope. "It's from Bizmark Productions."

"I guess it's my check," Jenny said.

"You don't sound very excited," said Mrs. Archer. "If I got a check for five hundred dollars, I'd be thrilled."

Jenny tore open the envelope. She unfolded the letter inside. A narrow green piece of paper fluttered to the floor.

Dear Miss Archer,

We think you will be pleased to know that your commercial for Nibble, Nibble

Gerbil Kibble is a great success. It was a test commercial. We have been showing it only in this area.

But the Nibble, Nibble Company loved your natural enthusiasm and charming personality. Therefore they have decided to broadcast the commercial throughout the entire United States.

Because your commercial will be used nationwide, your payment has been raised. Congratulations! We hope you have fun with the extra money.

Sincerely,
Arthur Mark
Bizmark Productions

Mrs. Archer was holding the green piece of paper. "Jenny"—her voice sounded shaky—"this check is for nine hundred dollars. I thought you were only getting five hundred."

"*Nine hundred dollars!*" Jenny shrieked. She took the check from her mother.

"Why did they pay you so much?" Mrs. Archer asked.

Jenny handed her mother the letter. She stared at the check. PAY TO THE ORDER OF JENNY ARCHER: $900 (NINE HUNDRED DOLLARS).

"I'm going to faint!" she screamed, and flopped down on the floor. But she held on to the check.

Nine hundred dollars! That was almost a thousand dollars. For less than five minutes on TV!

Barkley trotted over to her and licked her ear. He sat down beside her. She held out the check. "See, Barkley?" Jenny whispered it because she could hardly breathe. "It really says nine hundred dollars."

Barkley poked his nose against the check, as if he wanted to read it himself.

"I can buy you a lot of Bow-Wow Burgers with nine hundred dollars," Jenny promised.

Barkley pricked up his ears. He didn't know anything about money. But he knew what Bow-Wow Burgers were.

"And a pony," Jenny said. "A lot of Bow-Wow Burgers and a pony."

"This is incredible." Jenny's mother folded up the letter. "They really loved you."

"Nine hundred dollars for five minutes," Jenny said. She was still lying on the floor. "And if I did one commercial a week . . . fifty-two weeks a year . . . that's almost *fifty-two thousand dollars a year!*"

She leapt up from the floor and flung the check into the air. *"Yes!"* she cried.

"But Jenny"—her mother caught the check as it floated down—"I thought you were never going to make another commercial."

Jenny began to twirl around the room like a reckless ballerina. "That's what I thought, too," she said. "But I was really angry when I said that." She twirled around the coffee table.

"I can see you're not angry anymore," her mother said.

"How can I stay angry at people who like me so much?" Jenny asked. "How can I stay angry at people who *pay* me so much?" She twirled around an armchair.

"Money isn't everything, Jenny," said Mrs. Archer. "If you think a product is bad, do you want to tell people to buy it?"

Jenny stopped twirling.

"Oh, no. I'd only do honest commercials. For good things." Her eyes lit up. "Things like pizza, and sugarless bubble gum, and pony chow."

She jumped onto the armchair. She put her hand over her heart, as if she were reciting the Pledge of Allegiance.

"And no matter how much they pay me," she said, "I will never, *ever* do a commercial for anchovies."

The First Chapter in a Lifetime of Reading

Howling for Home by Joan Carris

All Star Fever by Matt Christopher

Centerfield Ballhawk by Matt Christopher

The Hit-Away Kid by Matt Christopher

The Lucky Baseball Bat by Matt Christopher

Man Out at First by Matt Christopher

The Spy on Third Base by Matt Christopher

Zero's Slider by Matt Christopher

Can Do, Jenny Archer by Ellen Conford

A Case for Jenny Archer by Ellen Conford

Get the Picture, Jenny Archer? by Ellen Conford

Jenny Archer, Author by Ellen Conford

Nibble, Nibble, Jenny Archer by Ellen Conford

What's Cooking, Jenny Archer? by Ellen Conford

Wonder Kid Meets the Evil Lunch Snatcher by Lois Duncan

The Monsters of Marble Avenue by Linda Gondosch

Happy Burpday, Maggie McDougal! by Valiska Gregory

Song of the Giraffe by Shannon K. Jacobs

A Dragon in the Family by Jackie French Koller

B.J.'s Billion-Dollar Bet by Julie Anne Peters

The Stinky Sneakers Contest by Julie Anne Peters

The Bathwater Gang by Jerry Spinelli

The Bathwater Gang Gets Down to Business by Jerry Spinelli